The Hunters
Predators of the Animal Kingdom

Written by Octavio Pintos
Illustrated by Martín Iannuzzi

Translated from Spanish by Juan Diego Otero

Printed by Agpograf, Barcelona, Spain
Made in Europe

Published by Little Gestalten, Berlin, 2024
ISBN 978-3-96704-776-9

The Spanish original edition, Cazadores—notas sobre cómo cazan
las especies, was published by Mosquito Books Barcelona
© Mosquito Books Barcelona, 2024
© Author: Octavio Pintos, 2024
© Illustrations: Martín Iannuzzi, 2024
© For the English edition: Little Gestalten, an imprint of
Die Gestalten Verlag GmbH & Co. KG, Berlin, 2024

For more information, and to order books, please visit
gestalten.com/collections/little-gestalten

Bibliographic information published by the
Deutsche Nationalbibliothek.
The Deutsche Nationalbibliothek lists this publication
in the Deutsche Nationalbibliografie;
detailed bibliographic data are available online at dnb.de.

This book was printed on paper certified according to the
standards of the FSC®.

THE HUNTERS

PREDATORS OF THE ANIMAL KINGDOM

OCTAVIO PINTOS • MARTÍN IANNUZZI

LITTLE GESTALTEN

OBSERVE AND DISCOVER

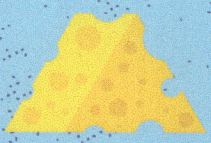

By land, sea, and air, alone or in groups, lying in wait or pursuing their prey—some of our planet's predators have become formidable hunters to survive in the wild.

In the animal kingdom, each species has developed its own methods for capturing its prey. Hunting techniques can be very different and are connected with the animal's adaptation to the ecosystem in which they live, their anatomy, the development of their senses, and the way they live.

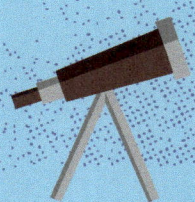

In this book, you will discover a diverse range of animals that live in different regions and landscapes across our planet. Our world has so many known and yet-to-be-discovered species that it would be impossible to cover them all in a single book.

CONTENTS

HOW TO READ THIS BOOK

HABITAT
The place where each animal lives.

LIFE EXPECTANCY
How long an animal usually lives.

MEASUREMENTS
Information on the size, weight, or height of the animal (or other specific characteristics).

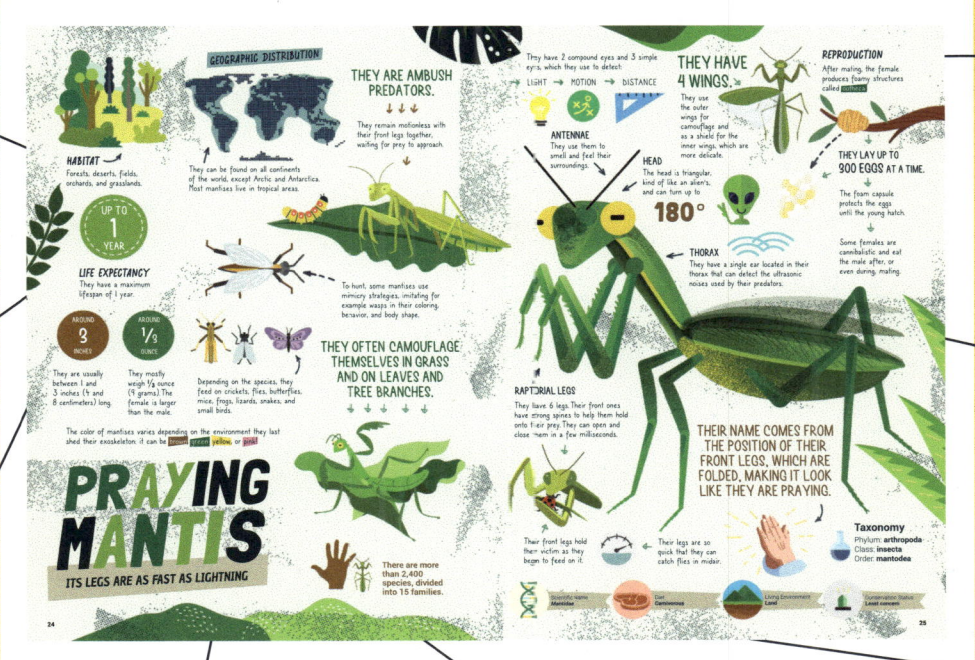

REPRODUCTION
How the species generates its offspring.

HUNTING BEHAVIOR
This gives you information about the hunting techniques of each animal.

INTERESTING FACT
Some extra information about each animal.

GEOGRAPHICAL DISTRIBUTION
These color patches on the map show you the geographical area where the animal lives.

ANTHROPOMETRIC SCALE
Size comparison between the animal and a person who is 5 feet 7 inches (1.7 meters) tall.

SIGNS AND SYMBOLS

TAXONOMY
(Classification of living organisms)

Phylum
A major taxonomic group of living beings, positioned above a class and below a kingdom.

Class
Phyla are divided into classes based on the most common characteristics among them.

Order
An order is based on common characteristics among its members that are more specific than those that define a class.

CONSERVATION STATUS

Least concern
The conservation category for animals considered not at risk of extinction.

Vulnerable
The conservation category for animals that are at a high risk of extinction.

Endangered
The conservation category for animals that are at the highest risk of extinction.

DIET TYPE

Omnivorous
Refers to animals that feed on both plants and meat.

Carnivorous
Refers to animals that feed mostly on meat.

SCIENTIFIC NAME

Scientific Name
The Latin name given to every living or extinct organism.

LIVING ENVIRONMENT

Air
Assigned to animals that can fly.

Water
Designates animals that live in oceans, seas, rivers, or lakes.

Land
Assigned to animals that live on land.

Land and water
Assigned to animals that live both on land and in water.

THEY HAVE 2 PINCERS AT THE FRONT AND 8 LEGS.

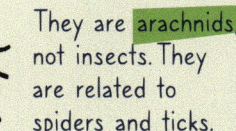

They are arachnids, not insects. They are related to spiders and ticks.

They hunt at night, grabbing their prey with their pincers and injecting them with venom from the stinger on their tail.

They can freeze during the night and then thaw out in the morning sun and walk away without any problems.

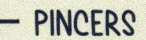

PINCERS
They have a pair of large front claws that are sometimes called pincers.

JAWS

They break down their prey with their jaws, which cover it in digestive fluids secreted by the intestine.

Their exoskeleton is made of chitin, which provides support, mobility, and protection.

This process liquefies the softer parts, which are then sucked into the stomach.

ABDOMEN
The front part of the body has 8 legs and is where you will find the eyes, brain, mouth, and oral chelicerae (mouth parts).

CEPHALOTHORAX
Ring-shaped segments that are flexibly connected to each other. This section contains the digestive and reproductive systems, the tail, and the stinger.

LEGS

8 inches
World's largest species.

1/3 inch
World's smallest species.

STINGER
Their stinger delivers the venom. It is used for self-defense or to kill prey.

THEY ARE OPPORTUNISTIC HUNTERS AND OFTEN CANNIBALS.

TAIL
Males are often thinner and have longer tails than females.

LIFE EXPECTANCY

UP TO 25 YEARS

Their lifespan ranges from 6 months to 25 years.

UP TO 1 OUNCE

They rarely weigh more than 1 ounce (28 grams).

AROUND 3 INCHES

The most common ones can reach between 2 and 3 inches (51 and 76 millimeters).

They have existed for over 350 million years—as far back as when dinosaurs roamed the Earth.

SCORPION
IT PARALYZES PREY WITH ITS STINGER

More than 2,000 species of scorpions have been discovered, but only 25 to 50 of them possess venom strong enough to kill a human.

They feed on insects, spiders, snails, lizards, snakes, rodents, and other scorpions.

They are able to slow down their metabolism when food is scarce.

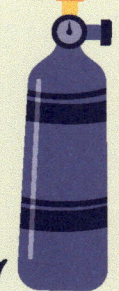

This technique allows them to reduce their oxygen consumption and live on a single insect per year. Even with their metabolism slowed, they are amazing hunters.

REPRODUCTION
THEY REPRODUCE DURING THE WARM MONTHS.

A male scorpion will lead a female scorpion in a sort of walk or dance, holding her by the pincers. They will sometimes even sting each other! The female attracts the male with special scents (pheromones).

THE FEMALE INCUBATES THE EGGS INSIDE HER BODY.

For some species it takes up to 12 months to give birth to live young.

Depending on the species she can have between 1 and 100 young at a time. The young climb onto the female's back until they can hunt and live on their own.

The color varies depending on their habitat. They can be yellow, light brown, dark brown, or black.

ARID ZONE
It can run quickly over sand and does not dry out.

ROCKY ZONE
They have flat bodies that allow them to slide through holes and cracks.

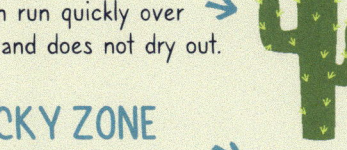

CAVE ZONE
They make or find burrows underground. They only emerge to hunt and reproduce.

THEY STAY COMPLETELY STILL UNTIL THEY CAN AMBUSH (SURPRISE ATTACK) THEIR PREY.

- They locate prey through vibrations in the ground.
- They detect vibrations made by insects and spiders.
- They can determine the distance and exact direction of their prey.

Taxonomy

Phylum: **arthropoda**
Class: **arachnida**
Order: **scorpiones**

GEOGRAPHIC DISTRIBUTION

Scorpions can be found in all parts of the world, except Greenland and Antarctica. Their habitat extends from North America to South America, Central Europe, North Africa, South Africa, the Middle East, and southern Asia.

HABITAT

Deserts, grasslands, savannas, prairies, and forests in temperate, subtropical, and tropical climates.

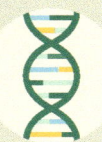
Scientific Name
Scorpiones

Diet
Carnivorous

Living Environment
Land

Conservation Status
Least concern

WOLF
IT HUNTS IN PACKS

There are 32 subspecies of wolves, grouped into 4 classes: white, gray, red, and brown.

WOLVES HAVE EXCELLENT VISION IN LOW LIGHT

Their fur is thick and consists of 2 layers designed to repel water and dirt and insulate them from the elements.

The color of their fur corresponds to their habitat; they take on their coloring as a form of camouflage.

They can howl to indicate their location and to rally the pack. Group howling strengthens their social bonds. They often howl in the evenings, and it is common for adult wolves to howl when they go out to hunt.

They have a keen sense of hearing and can perceive sounds at both high and low frequencies.

Their sense of smell is extraordinary: they can smell their prey long before they can see it.

NIGHT VISION
This ability is due to a layer of tissue behind the retina that allows it to capture more light when it is dark.

UP TO 13 YEARS

LIFE EXPECTANCY
Their life expectancy is 8 to 13 years.

The first fossil records date back 800,000 years.

Taxonomy
Phylum: **chordata**
Class: **mammalia**
Order: **carnivora**

HABITAT
They live in different ecosystems around the world, from the Arctic tundra to forests, meadows, and arid landscapes.

GEOGRAPHICAL DISTRIBUTION

They can be found in a number of locations within Europe, Asia, and North America.

ALMOST 5 FEET

They can reach almost 5 feet (1.5 meters) in length.

UP TO 154 POUNDS

Wolves can weigh between 90 and 154 pounds (41 and 70 kilograms). Females usually weigh 20 percent less than males.

REPRODUCTION
The gestation period of wolves is about 60 to 63 days.

THEIR LITTERS USUALLY HAVE BETWEEN 2 AND 6 PUPS.

At birth a pup can weigh up to about 1 pound (0.5 kilograms). They are born blind, deaf, and entirely dependent on their mother.

At 7 months, the wolf pups are referred to as wolf cubs. After 3 years, the cubs leave their birth pack.

THEY HAVE A PRONOUNCED JAW THAT IS DESIGNED TO GRAB, HOLD, AND PIERCE THEIR PREY.

THEY ARE VERY TERRITORIAL. THEY ATTACK BY SURPRISE AND STALK THEIR PREY FOR HOURS.

They organize into packs with a strict social hierarchy led by an alpha male and an alpha female.

They are nocturnal predators, hunting for food at night and resting during the day.

Their diet consists of large herbivores and other smaller mammals. They also sometimes eat wild berries. They consume almost 9 pounds (4 kilograms) of food per day.

They attack their prey from behind and kill it with a bite to the throat.

↓ ↓ ↓

They use their teeth to pull apart the meat and crush the bones of their prey.

The pack maintains its order. When they launch an attack, they growl and snarl.

UP TO 20 INCHES

Their tails measure between 13 and 20 inches (33 and 51 centimeters)

They have non-retractable claws that allow them to grip the surfaces as they run the different terrains of their habitats.

They use their claws for climbing, digging, gripping while running, and sometimes catching their prey.

6 MPH

They can cover several miles, trotting at a speed of around 6 mph (10 km/h)

↓ ↓ ↓

When hunting, they can reach speeds of 40 mph (64 km/h).

His hind paws are bigger than his front paws.

They have a gland at the base of their tail that leaves a trail with a unique scent, which they use to identify each other.

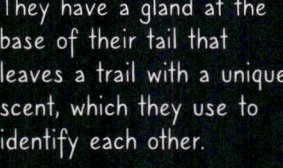

 Scientific Name
Canis lupus

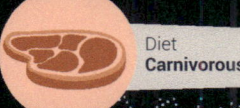 Diet
Carnivorous

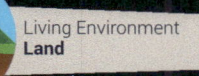 Living Environment
Land

 Conservation Status
Vulnerable

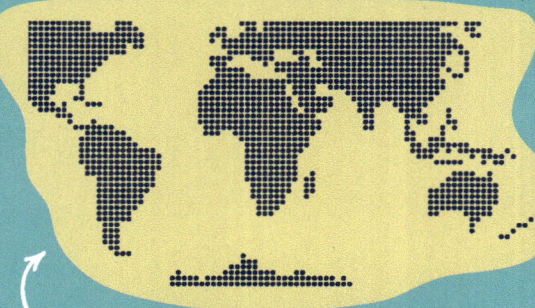

HABITAT
Coastal and oceanic waters.

THEIR BACK IS BLACK. THEIR CHEST, BELLY, AND SIDES ARE WHITE. THEY ALSO HAVE A WHITE PATCH BEHIND THEIR EYES.

They can be found in all the oceans of the world and in most of the seas—sometimes even in the Mediterranean and occasionally in the Red Sea.

They have excellent vision, both inside and outside the water. Their hearing is highly developed and they have an advanced sense of touch.

Orcas can imitate human and animal sounds, learn new behaviors, and even solve tasks.

They have a system of echolocation capable of detecting the position and size of their prey.

DORSAL FIN

They have very strong jaw muscles with a bite that's stronger than a great white shark's.

MELON

EYESPOT

SNOUT

The dorsal fin is their distinguishing feature. It differs in size, shape and number of scars on each animal.

40–56

They have between 40 and 56 teeth, all with the same shape.

PECTORAL FINS

LIFE EXPECTANCY

UP TO **30** YEARS

Males live to be about 30 years old on average.

UP TO **35** MPH

Their strength and hydrodynamic shape make them one of the fastest marine mammals.

UP TO **32** FEET

Males measure up to 32 feet (9.75 meters), females up to 28 feet (8.5 meters).

UP TO **14,500** POUNDS

Males can weigh up to 14,500 pounds (6,600 kilograms). Females weigh between 6,600 and 8,800 pounds (3,000 and 4,000 kilograms).

Scientific Name
Orcinus orca

Diet
Carnivorous

Living Environment
Water

Conservation Status
Locally vulnerable

THEY ARE AN APEX PREDATOR OF THE OCEAN.

220–440 lbs

They consume 220 to 440 pounds (100 to 200 kilograms) of food daily.

Their diet varies by region. They can feed on birds, fish, and mammals.

They emit sounds to orient themselves, to locate food, and to communicate. They produce three types of sounds:

→ TONAL WHISTLES
→ ECHOLOCATION CLICKS
→ MODULAR CALLS

Sometimes they hunt by pursuing their prey until they give up out of exhaustion.

◄ **TAIL FIN**
They emit sounds and slap their tails to stun their prey and disorient them.

They sometimes drive their prey into the shallow water on the shores and even create waves to knock mammals resting on small icebergs into the water.

THEY ARE EXCELLENT HUNTERS AND CAN HUNT ALONE OR IN PACKS.

⇓ ⇓ ⇓

They finish off their prey by biting.

REPRODUCTION
ORCAS MATE WITH SEVERAL PARTNERS.

The gestation period of the calf is between 15 and 17 months.

→ They give birth to a single calf that measures about 8 feet (2.4 meters) in length and weighs 440 pounds (200 kilograms).

→ The mortality rate of calves is high during the first 6 months of life, with a death rate of between **37% and 50%.**

BELLY SPOT

Taxonomy
Phylum: **chordata**
Class: **mammalia**
Order: **cetacea**

THERE ARE 3 TYPES OF ORCAS IN THE NORTH PACIFIC WATERS

Residents: Do not migrate. They live in in family groups of up to 5 generations. Their dorsal fin is curved and rounded at the tip.

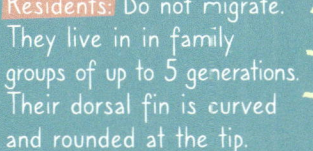

Transients: Move in small groups or on their own. They are in constant motion. They have a triangular dorsal fin with a pointed tip.

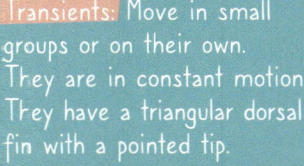

Marine: Move in the open seas in groups of up to 50 individuals. They are smaller than other orcas. Their dorsal fin is similar to that of resident orcas.

ORCA
AN EFFECTIVE HUNTER

It belongs to the dolphin family.

EAGLE
SILENT AND POWERFUL

There are 10 species in the genus of white-tailed eagle, but also many other eagle species.

Eagles are birds of prey that hunt during the day. They prefer to hunt in open spaces with good visibility.

Their beaks curve downward, forming a kind of hook with sharp edges.

Together with their claws, their beak allows them to tear apart the flesh of their prey.

They use their claws to strangle their prey and take it to a safe place.

TO CATCH THEIR PREY, THEY SWOOP DOWN AND GRAB IT IN THEIR STRONG CLAWS.

They eat carrion (the flesh of dead animals) and animals such as rabbits, rodents, lizards, snakes, and fish, as well as other, smaller birds.

They have a fairly small stomach: they can only eat about 1 pound (0.5 kilograms) of food per day.

They have a pouch in their throat called a crop, where they store food until there is room in their stomach to digest it.

REPRODUCTION
THEY ARE MONOGAMOUS BIRDS, WHICH MEANS THEY HAVE THE SAME PARTNER FOR LIFE.

Male and female eagles perform a courtship flight to strengthen their bond. They look for tall trees or rocky cliffs and build their nest in the same place every year.

THE FEMALE USUALLY LAYS 2 EGGS.

The male and female take turns incubating the eggs until they hatch, which happens, depending on the species, between 30 and 45 days later.

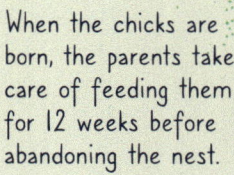

When the chicks are born, the parents take care of feeding them for 12 weeks before abandoning the nest.

LIFE EXPECTANCY

UP TO 30 YEARS

Their life expectancy ranges on average between 15 and 30 years.

HABITAT
Arid, semi-arid, and mountainous areas with temperate forests. They can also live in mountains near valleys, on mountain slopes, in ravines, and in meadows.

GEOGRAPHIC DISTRIBUTION

They can be found in Europe, Asia, Africa, America, and Australia.

Taxonomy
Phylum: **chordata**
Class: **aves**
Order: **accipitriformes**

Their eyes have two focal points, one for looking straight ahead and the other for looking off to the side at the same time.

Their vision is extremely sharp and allows them to see prey from more than a mile (1.6 kilometers) away.

THEY HAVE LONG, BROAD WINGS.

When flying, they keep their wings still and firm.

UP TO 36 INCHES

Depending on the species, the length of its body ranges from 16 to 36 inches (40 to 91 centimeters).

MORE THAN 6 FEET

The largest eagles can have a wingspan of more than 6 feet (1.8 meters).

UP TO 20 POUNDS

Their weight varies depending on the species: between 4 and 20 pounds (1.8 and 9.1 kilograms). Females are much larger than males.

They mark their territory with calls, warning other eagles that they are in their space.

THEY CAN FLY AT SPEEDS OF UP TO 200 MPH WHILE DIVING.

THEY CAN REACH AN ALTITUDE OF OVER **9,800 FEET (3,000 METERS)** ABOVE SEA LEVEL.

FEATHERS

Their feathers are often dark on the outside to blend in with plants and light on the inside to blend in with the sky.

THEIR TALONS ALLOW THEM TO LIFT ANIMALS THAT ARE UP TO 4 TIMES HEAVIER THAN THEMSELVES.

Their legs are strong and muscular, with large, sharp claws.

Depending on the species, they can be dark brown, gray, or white.

Their tail is quite distinctive. Some of them have a rounded shape with the tip pointing outward.

Scientific Name **Aquila**

Diet **Carnivorous**

Living Environment **Air**

Conservation Status **Endangered**

POLAR BEAR
THE HUNTER OF THE ICY NORTH

Scientists have identified 19 populations living in 5 different sea ice regions in the Arctic.

They are very fast at capturing their prey. When animals open holes in the ice to breathe, they grab them with their claws.

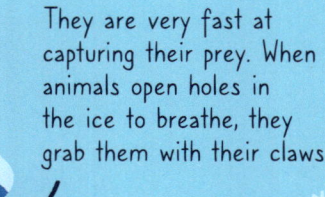

They have brown eyes and a third eyelid that protects their eyes from UV radiation.

Like other bears, the polar bear can stand upright and even walk over short distances.

Taxonomy
Phylum: **chordata**
Class: **mammalia**
Order: **carnivora**

Polar bears use their sense of smell to track seal pups sheltered in chambers under the ice.

GEOGRAPHIC DISTRIBUTION

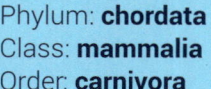

They can be found in the Arctic region, in Canada, Alaska, Greenland, Iceland, Russia, and Svalbard (Spitsbergen, Norway).

Light reflects various tones in their fur, such as white, light brown, yellow, and gray.

They have well-developed legs for walking and swimming long distances.

HABITAT
Frozen Arctic waters, open seasonal waters in summer, and regions of dry land in the Arctic tundra.

They have thick, short, and pointed claws, measuring 3.5 to 6 inches (9 to 15 centimeters) in length, allowing them to easily grip ice floes.

They live in temperatures ranging from –58° F in winter to 32° F in summer (–50 °C to 0 °C).

They feed on ringed and bearded seals, young walruses, seabirds, and fish.

They have 42 teeth and a very strong bite.

They can climb on icy and hard-to-reach terrain.

REPRODUCTION

Their mating season is between April and May.

The cubs stay with their mother for 2 to 3 years.

Polar bears are pregnant for about 8 months and usually have litters of 2 cubs.

The cubs weigh about 1 pound (0.5 kilograms) and measure up to 12 inches (30 centimeters).

LIFE EXPECTANCY

UP TO 30 YEARS

Their life expectancy in the wild is 25 to 30 years.

UP TO 2,200 POUNDS

Males weigh 660 to 2,200 pounds (300 to 1,000 kilograms).

UP TO 10 FEET

They measure between 6 and 10 feet (1.8 and 3 meters) when standing up. Females are smaller, measuring up to about 6 feet (1.8 meters).

In their search for food, they can get trapped on drifting ice floes.

In summer, when the ice melts, bears survive on the fat reserves stored in their bodies.

Under their translucent fur, their skin is black. It absorbs the sun's rays and increases body heat.

They can swim at a speed of about 6 miles per hour (9.7 kilometers per hour).

Scientific Name
Ursus maritimus

Diet
Carnivcrous

Living Environment
Water and land

Conservation Status
Vulnerable

MORE THAN
6
FEET

They have a slender body that allows them to climb trees and swim in rivers.

They have round, black eyes with limited visual ability.

EYES

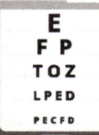

They can reach more than 6 feet (1.8 meters) in length.

In the front part of their jaw, they have hollow fangs that they use to inject venom into their victims.

UP TO
13
POUNDS

A small amount of its venom can kill 20 humans or 1 elephant.

They can weigh up to 13 pounds (5.9 kilograms). Males are usually larger than females.

THEIR VENOM IS TOXIC AND POWERFUL.

A single bite paralyzes their prey and eventually leads to respiratory and cardiac arrest.

They are also known as the "spectacled cobra" due to a pair of spots resembling glasses on the back of their hood.

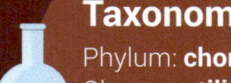

Their skin is formed by smooth scales that overlap in diagonal rows.

The color of their scales varies: they have brown, green, gray, yellow, reddish, and black tones.

INDIAN COBRA

ITS VENOM IS LETHAL

Taxonomy
Phylum: **chordata**
Class: **reptilia**
Order: **squamata**

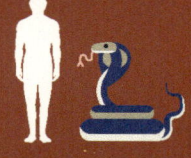

More than 34 species of true cobras have been identified so far.

Their head is small, elongated, and flat.

When they feel threatened or agitated, they adopt a defensive posture by raising a third of their body and spreading their neck hood and hissing at the same time.

In attack mode, they spread their neck hood, attack their prey, and bite. Then they wait for the venom to take effect.

THEY GO HUNTING AT NIGHT.

They use their forked tongues to collect odor molecules in the air, which provide information for them to locate their prey, detect the presence of predators, and distinguish between males and females.

The neck hood unfurls around the head. It is formed by a thin layer of skin attached to their ribs.

THEY HAVE FLEXIBLE JAWS THAT ALLOW THEM TO SWALLOW THEIR PREY IN ONE BITE.

They eat once a week and feed on rodents, toads, frogs, birds, and other snakes.

REPRODUCTION

They lay

10-30 EGGS.

The female snake lays up to 30 white eggs.

Incubation lasts between 48 and 69 days, depending on the temperature.

The offspring are independent and are born measuring

8-12 INCHES
(20 TO 30 CENTIMETERS).

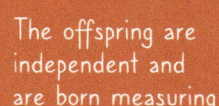

They hide in burrows, termite mounds, under rocks, or in holes in trees.

GEOGRAPHIC DISTRIBUTION

They can be found mostly in India, Pakistan, Sri Lanka, Bangladesh, Nepal, and southern China.

LIFE EXPECTANCY

UP TO 25 YEARS

Their life expectancy is up to 25 years.

HABITAT

Open fields, jungles, densely vegetated forests, riverine areas, and arid and semi-arid regions.

 Scientific Name **Naja naja**

 Diet **Carnivorous**

 Living Environment **Land**

 Conservation Status **Least concern**

TASMANIAN DEVIL

FEROCIOUS AND SCARY

THEY HAVE THE STRONGEST BITE RELATIVE TO THEIR WEIGHT OF ANY MAMMAL ON THE PLANET.

The name **TASMANIAN DEVIL** comes from their carnivorous ferocity and their ears, which can resemble reddish horns in the sunlight.

They have long whiskers on their face and on top of their head that help them locate prey in the dark or detect other members of their species.

80° →

They can open their jaw to an angle of 80° and chomp down hard, tearing flesh and crushing bones.

UP TO 12 INCHES
They can grow up to 12 inches (30 centimeters) in height.

UP TO 26 INCHES
They can reach up to 26 inches (66 centimeters) in length.

UP TO 18 POUNDS
Males can weigh up to 18 pounds (8.2 kilograms), while females are smaller.

UP TO 8 MPH
They can run at a speed of 8 miles per hour (13 kilometers per hour).

Their front limbs have paws with 5 digits and are longer than the back ones.

The strength of their sharp teeth and long claws enables them to hunt large animals.

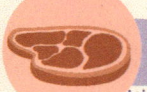
Scientific Name
Sarcophilus harrisii

Diet
Carnivorous

Living Environment
Land

Conservation Status
Endangered

They have excellent hearing and a keen sense of smell, able to detect prey up to 1 mile (1.6 kilometers) away.

1 mile

When threatened, they growl, lunge, and bare their teeth. They also have a shrill and frightening scream.

They hunt during the night and can travel up to 10 miles (16 kilometers) a day to catch prey.

10 miles

THEIR BODY IS ROBUST AND MUSCULAR, WITH A LARGE HEAD AND NECK.

They have black fur with irregular white patches on the chest and back.

THEY EAT IN GROUPS OF UP TO 12.

Tasmanian devils usually hunt alone, but eat in community.

They feed on mammals such as small kangaroos, wombats, sheep and rats, but also on birds, fish, frogs, insects, snakes, and carrion.

The tail, which measures half the length of the body, functions as a stabilizer when running.

They have a scent gland at the base of their tail to mark their territory.

WHEN THEY FEEL THREATENED, THEY EMIT A STRONG AND INTENSE SMELL.

UP TO 8 YEARS

LIFE EXPECTANCY

They can live up to 5 years in the wild and up to 8 years in captivity.

REPRODUCTION

The males fight for the female in order to mate.

21

GESTATION LASTS 21 DAYS.

They have 20 to 30 offspring at a time. At birth, the young must compete to get into their mother's pouch and cling to one of her 4 nipples.

ONLY 4 WILL SURVIVE

The young stay in their mother's pouch for about 77 days. At the age of 11 weeks, they ride on their mother's back until they can walk independently after 90 days.

GEOGRAPHIC DISTRIBUTION

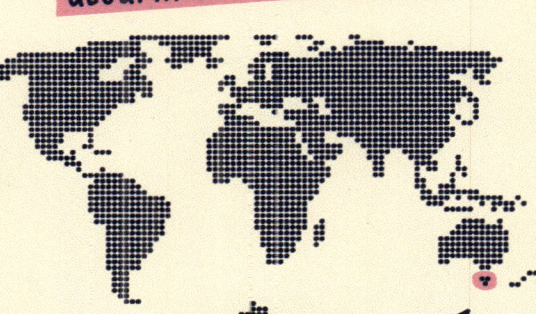

HABITAT

Can be found only on the island of Tasmania, south of the Australian mainland

Open fields with shrubs, bushland, coastal areas, and suburban areas.

Taxonomy

Phylum: **chordata**
Class: **mammalia**
Order: **dasyuromorphia**

ELECTRIC EELS CAN EMIT ELECTRIC SHOCKS OF UP TO 860 VOLTS.

10
TO A GROUP
They hunt in groups of up to 10.

They have 3 organs that produce electric shocks of different intensity:

→ MAIN ORGAN
→ HUNTER'S ORGAN
→ SACHS'S ORGAN

UP TO 44 POUNDS

They can weigh up to 44 pounds (20 kilograms).

UP TO 8 FEET

They can measure up to 8 feet (2.4 meters) in length.

They coil around their prey to double the power of the shock, bringing the two poles of their electric organ together.

HABITAT →
Calm waters—they prefer muddy beds, streams, rivers, and swampy areas.

GEOGRAPHIC DISTRIBUTION

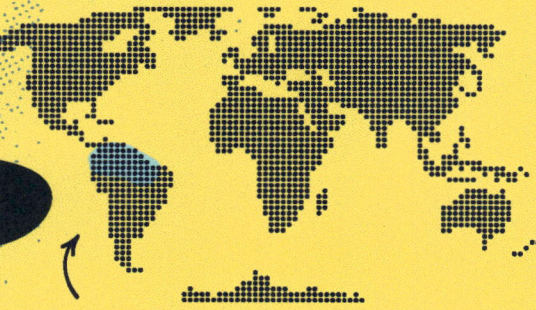

They can be found in the northern regions of South America, the Orinoco River basin, the Amazon River basin, and their adjacent rivers.

They corner fish and deliver brief, high-voltage shocks as a team. Once their prey is immobilized, they devour it.

They can generate up to 8 high-voltage shocks within 2-3 milliseconds—up to 150 in one hour!

THEY ARE THE MOST POWERFUL BIOELECTRIC BEING ON THE PLANET.

Like all fish, they have the ability to regulate their body temperature in response to the water.

ELECTRIC EELs
IT SHOCKS ITS PREY

They are an electric fish that resemble a snake, and there are 3 known species.

THEY USE THE DARK OF NIGHT TO HUNT.

OVER 20 YEARS

LIFE EXPECTANCY

Only known in captivity: females can live for over 20 years, males up to 15 years.

Their eyes are small and they have poor vision, but they have a keen sense of smell.

They use their tail fin to move.

Their bodies house more than 6,000 specialized cells called electrocytes, which are able to store energy.

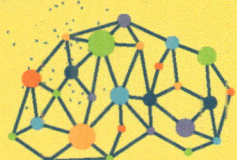

They feed on fish, small mammals, and birds.

The color of their skin varies between gray and dark brown on the back and yellow or orange on the belly.

They have a flat head and a large mouth, with a row of cone-shaped teeth in the lower jaw.

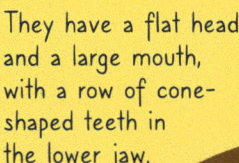

Their skin is oily, sticky, and has no scales.

REPRODUCTION

The male builds a nest out of foam and aquatic plants.

The female lays

17,000 EGGS.

Newly born eels eat small invertebrates.

Up to 3,000 young are born each time.

THEY CAN REACH A SPEED OF 5 MILES PER HOUR (8 KILOMETERS PER HOUR).

ANAL FIN

They have an elongated anal fin that extends to the tip of their tail.

Taxonomy

Phylum: **chordata**
Class: **actinopterygii**
Order: **gymnotiformes**

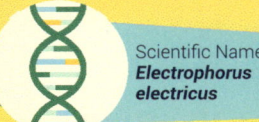

Scientific Name
Electrophorus electricus

Diet
Carnivorous

Living Environment
Water

Conservation Status
Least concern

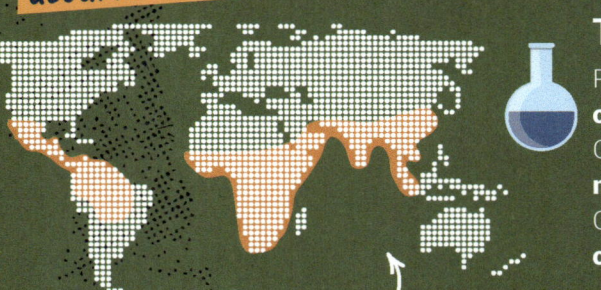

Taxonomy

Phylum:
chordata
Class:
mammalia
Order:
carnivora

LIFE EXPECTANCY

UP TO
17
YEARS

Their life expectancy is 12 to 17 years in the wild, depending on the species.

HABITAT

Forests, open fields, savannas, and densely vegetated jungle.

As leopards they can be found in Africa and southeastern Asia; as jaguars they can be found in Central America and the north of South America.

JAGUARS AND LEOPARDS ARE AMONG THE 5 BIGGEST CATS IN THE WORLD.

Their eyes can be green, blue, yellow, or gold.

They have excellent night vision.

Their slit pupils adapt to the surrounding light.

Their color is due to an overabundance of a dark brown to black pigment (melanin), which makes their fur appear black.

Their distinctive spots blend in with their dark fur. Each animal has unique spots.

UP TO
200
POUNDS

They can weigh up to 200 pounds (91 kilograms). Females are smaller than males.

UP TO
5
FEET

They measure up to 5 feet (1.5 meters) in length.

UP TO
3
FEET

They are approximately 3 feet (0.9 meters) tall.

LEGS

Their short, muscular legs give them strength and grip.

They have retractable claws that can be deployed as needed.

PANTHER

IT STRIKES SILENTLY

A panther can be a leopard or a jaguar. These are two different species that look very similar.

THEY HUNT ALONE, IN THE DARKNESS OF THE NIGHT.

Leopards have a small head and a large jaw, with sharp teeth and fangs, ready to attack their prey.

REPRODUCTION

Leopards and jaguars are solitary animals and only meet to mate.

THEIR GESTATION PERIOD LASTS 3 TO 4 MONTHS.

They move slowly and cautiously.

Their dark coloring helps them to blend in with dense forests, where light levels are low.

It also protects against excessive sunlight.

They spend many hours a day licking their fur to remove any trace of scent left by their prey.

THEY GIVE BIRTH TO UP TO 4 CUBS IN EACH LITTER.

The cubs remain with their mother for 2 years.

They move about within a radius of 25 miles (40 kilometers) to search for food.

They hunt cautiously and can wait for hours to launch their surprise attack.

10 ft
They can jump more than 10 feet (3 meters) in the air.

50 mph
A jaguar can sprint at speeds of up to 50 mph (80 km/h), a leopard up to 37 mph (60 km/h).

UP TO 39 INCHES

Their tail measures between 18 and 39 inches (46 and 99 centimeters) in length.

Depending on the species, they feed on tapirs, rabbits, capybaras, antelopes, deer, fish, lizards, and birds.

They climb trees to rest, stalk, shelter, and eat.

Scientific Names
Panthera pardus
Panthera onca

Diet
Carnivorous

Living Environment
Land

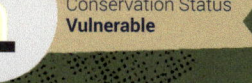
Conservation Status
Vulnerable

21

HERON

ITS BEAK NEVER MISSES

There are more than 60 species worldwide.

UP TO 5 POUNDS

Their average weight is between 1 and 5 pounds (0.5 and 2.3 kilograms).

UP TO 25 YEARS

LIFE EXPECTANCY

Their life expectancy is 25 years.

They are sedentary. Some species migrate to warmer climates for the winter.

UP TO 5 FEET

They can grow up to 5 feet (1.5 meters) tall.

Their tails are short and their wings are long and broad.

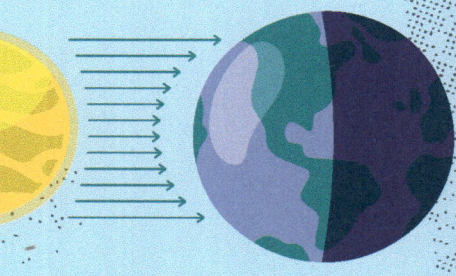

MORE THAN 7 FEET

Their wingspan can measure more than 7 feet (2.1 meters).

LEGS

Their legs are long, thin, and black.

GEOGRAPHIC DISTRIBUTION

They can be found on all continents except the Arctic and Antarctic regions.

HABITAT

Swamps, flooded farmland, mangroves, coastal regions, and near lakes, lagoons, and rivers.

On their middle toe, they have a structure similar to a comb that they use to groom their feathers.

Taxonomy

Phylum: **chordata**
Class: **aves**
Order: **pelecaniformes**

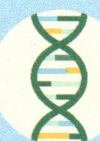
Scientific Name
Ardeidae

Diet
Carnivorous

Living Environment
Air

Conservation Status
Least concern

THEY SPEND MOST OF THEIR TIME IN WATER

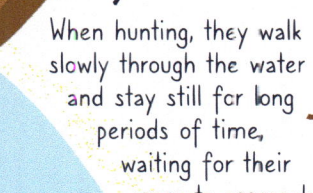

They have highly developed senses of hearing and touch, so that they can perceive their surroundings.

They make shrill noises when they feel threatened.

When hunting, they walk slowly through the water and stay still for long periods of time, waiting for their prey to approach.

They have sharp vision, and can calculate the exact angle at which their prey is located under the water.

They shake floating plants with their feet to scare fish and amphibians out of their hiding places.

When flying, they bend their neck and stretch their legs backwards.

They have a long, S-shaped neck, with vertebrae that make it very flexible.

They are very intelligent: they can learn to modify their hunting methods by observing other birds.

When they see their prey, they shoot their neck out at high speed, making their beak act like a deadly arrow. And they never miss. Then they swallow their prey in one gulp.

"S"

BEAK

They have a long, straight, pointy beak, which is yellow or orange in color.

The coloring of their feathers differs from species to species. They are often black, brown, blue, gray, and white.

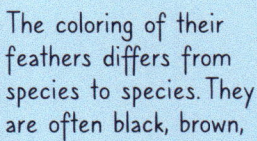

The bell heron spreads its wings like an umbrella. The fish are attracted to the shadow, thinking they are safe there, and then it strikes.

They feed on fish, amphibians, reptiles, and small mammals.

REPRODUCTION
HERONS ARE MONOGAMOUS.

They look for places near water to nest. They build their nests out of aquatic grasses and branches.

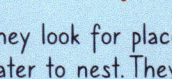

Some nest alone, others in colonies of their own species, and some even together with several other species.

THEY LAY UP TO 5 EGGS AT A TIME.

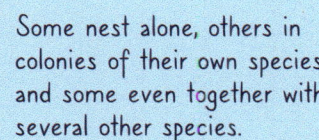

The eggs are incubated by the male and female for

25 days.

The chicks are born naked and are dependent on their parents for the first

7 weeks.

HABITAT
Forests, deserts, fields, orchards, and grasslands.

They can be found on all continents of the world, except Arctic and Antarctica. Most mantises live in tropical areas.

THEY ARE AMBUSH PREDATORS.

↓ ↓ ↓

They remain motionless with their front legs together, waiting for prey to approach.

UP TO 1 YEAR

LIFE EXPECTANCY
They have a maximum lifespan of 1 year.

To hunt, some mantises use mimicry strategies, imitating for example wasps in their coloring, behavior, and body shape.

AROUND 3 INCHES

AROUND 1/3 OUNCE

They are usually between 1 and 3 inches (4 and 8 centimeters) long.

They mostly weigh 1/3 ounce (9 grams). The female is larger than the male.

Depending on the species, they feed on crickets, flies, butterflies, mice, frogs, lizards, snakes, and small birds.

THEY OFTEN CAMOUFLAGE THEMSELVES IN GRASS AND ON LEAVES AND TREE BRANCHES.

The color of mantises varies depending on the environment they last shed their exoskeleton: it can be brown, green, yellow, or pink!

PRAYING MANTIS

ITS LEGS ARE AS FAST AS LIGHTNING

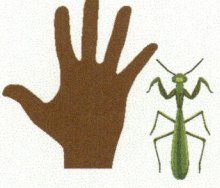

There are more than 2,400 species, divided into 15 families.

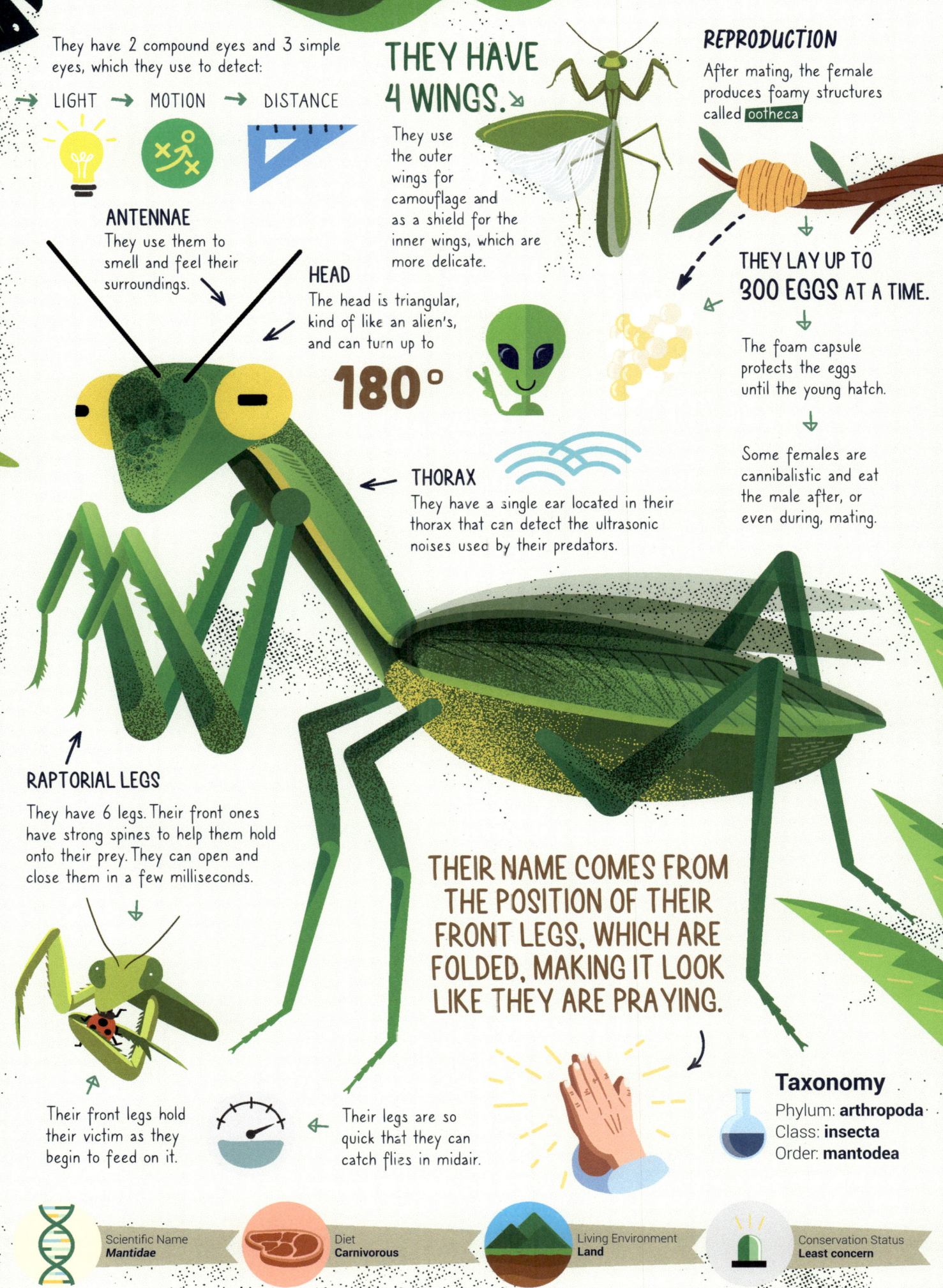

They have 2 compound eyes and 3 simple eyes, which they use to detect:

LIGHT → MOTION → DISTANCE

ANTENNAE
They use them to smell and feel their surroundings.

HEAD
The head is triangular, kind of like an alien's, and can turn up to

180°

THORAX
They have a single ear located in their thorax that can detect the ultrasonic noises used by their predators.

THEY HAVE 4 WINGS.
They use the outer wings for camouflage and as a shield for the inner wings, which are more delicate.

REPRODUCTION
After mating, the female produces foamy structures called ootheca

THEY LAY UP TO 300 EGGS AT A TIME.
The foam capsule protects the eggs until the young hatch.

Some females are cannibalistic and eat the male after, or even during, mating.

RAPTORIAL LEGS
They have 6 legs. Their front ones have strong spines to help them hold onto their prey. They can open and close them in a few milliseconds.

Their front legs hold their victim as they begin to feed on it.

Their legs are so quick that they can catch flies in midair.

THEIR NAME COMES FROM THE POSITION OF THEIR FRONT LEGS, WHICH ARE FOLDED, MAKING IT LOOK LIKE THEY ARE PRAYING.

Taxonomy
Phylum: **arthropoda**
Class: **insecta**
Order: **mantodea**

Scientific Name **Mantidae**

Diet **Carnivorous**

Living Environment **Land**

Conservation Status **Least concern**

CHIMPANZEE

IT CAN MAKE TOOLS TO HUNT WITH

There are 2 species—the common chimpanzee and the pygmy chimpanzee—and up to 4 subspecies have been identified.

They are the closest-living genetic relative to humans, with whom they share more than

95 %
of their DNA.

They make a wide variety of facial expressions.

Their cries and gestures allow them to communicate easily with each other.

It is believed that humans and chimpanzees share a common ancestor that lived between

7 and 13
million years ago.

THEY ARE SKILLED CLIMBERS.

Their body is covered in thick fur, except for the face, fingers, palms of the hands, and soles of the feet.

Taxonomy
Phylum: **chordata**
Class: **mammalia**
Order: **primates**

Their fur is dark brown or black in color.

They walk on all fours, with their fingers flexed, supporting their weight on their knuckles.

They only walk upright for short distances.

REPRODUCTION
They live in communities that can have between

15 AND 100 MEMBERS.

They are socially organized, with a dominant male and several females, along with their offspring.

Their gestation lasts

8 MONTHS.
Chimpanzees can weigh more than 4 pounds (1.8 kilograms) at birth.

The infant clings to its mother's fur. Weaning occurs between the ages of 4 and 5 years old.

ALMOST 6 FEET

They can reach a height of 6 feet (1.8 meters) when standing upright.

UP TO 155 POUNDS

Males can weigh between 77 and 155 pounds (35 and 70 kilograms).

UP TO 110 POUNDS

Females can weigh between 55 and 110 pounds (25 and 50 kilograms).

UP TO 40 YEARS

LIFE EXPECTANCY

They can live for up to 40 years.

They are able to hunt in organized groups, chasing their prey, catching and then dismembering it.

They poke leaves into termite mounds to fish them out, and use sticks to force insects out of their hiding places.

They build their nests in the treetops, where they rest in the middle of the day or sleep at night.

They usually hunt birds, small antelopes, monkeys, and even turtles, which they hit against trees to break their shells.

SOME CHIMPANZEES HUNT USING SHARPENED STICKS.

They sharpen them with their teeth and use them to kill small mammals that hide inside tree trunks.

They use stones to crack open nuts and use leaves as sponges to collect water.

↑ ↑ ↑ ↑ ↑ ↑ ↑ ↑ ↑ ↑

CHIMPANZEES ARE ONE OF THE FEW ANIMAL SPECIES THAT USE TOOLS TO HUNT FOR FOOD.

GEOGRAPHIC DISTRIBUTION

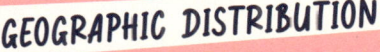

HABITAT

Tropical areas of rainforests, forests along rivers or on floodplains, and wooded savannas.

They can be found in the western and central regions of Africa.

They feed on fruit, plants, leaves, seeds, flowers, bark, resin, and roots. They also eat smaller amounts of insects, eggs, and small vertebrates.

Scientific Name
Pan troglodytes

Diet
Omnivorous

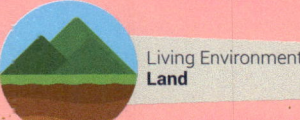
Living Environment
Land

Conservation Status
Endangered

They can dive to a depth of over 656 feet (200 meters) and stay underwater for 10 to 15 minutes.

They feed on fish, shrimp, squid, crabs, and mollusks.

THEY CAN CONSUME UP TO 7 POUNDS (3 KILOGRAMS) OF FOOD PER DAY.

7 LBS

31 mi

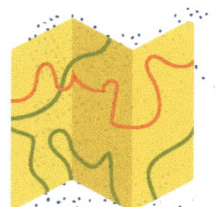

They travel up to 31 miles (50 kilometers) to catch their prey.

To orient themselves, they can detect objects with their whiskers by direct contact and analyze movements in the water.

THEY ARE EXCELLENT SWIMMERS.

They have sensory whiskers that help them detect vibrations underwater and find potential prey.

Their big, dark eyes allow them to see underwater at great depths, where there is little light.

UP TO 35 YEARS

LIFE EXPECTANCY
They can live for up to 35 years.

Leopard seals are relatives of the harbor seal family. They live in the Antarctic and hunt penguins, among other animals.

UP TO 350 POUNDS

They can weigh between 130 and 350 pounds (60 and 160 kilograms). Females are smaller than males.

THEY TRAP THEIR PREY WITH THEIR STRONG TEETH.

REPRODUCTION
The female digs a burrow as a shelter to give birth in.

THE GESTATION PERIOD IS 9 TO 11 MONTHS.

MORE THAN 6 FEET

The size varies depending on the species. They can grow to be well over 6 feet (1.8 meters) in length.

GEOGRAPHIC DISTRIBUTION

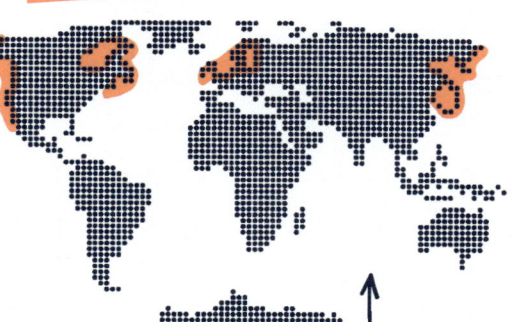

The pups weigh between
17 AND 26 POUNDS (8 AND 12 KILOGRAMS).

The pups will remain with their mother for 1 month.

Taxonomy
Phylum: **chordata**
Class: **mammalia**
Order: **carnivores**

HABITAT
Temperate and cold seas. Beaches, bays, and estuaries.

They can be found in coastal waters of the North Atlantic and Pacific oceans, the Baltic Sea, and the North Sea.

SEAL

IT DETECTS PREY WITH ITS WHISKERS

They are divided into more than 30 species, which look similar but live in different parts of the world.

ALSO KNOWN AS THE COMMON SEAL OR HARBOR SEAL.

Their fur is short and thick.

They have a small head with a flat nose, with curved nostrils shaped like the letter V.

They have sebaceous glands that release an oily substance to protect them from the sun's rays and keep their fur moist, which improves their agility when swimming.

They use their front flippers to maintain their course and their back flippers to propel themselves.

This allows them to maintain a healthy body temperature.

Their fur is gray, brown, or beige, with a pattern of dark spots that is different on every seal.

Their belly is always a lighter color than the rest of their body.

They have a long body that is perfectly adapted to swimming.

The front limbs are short and flat. The flippers are webbed and each have 5 digits that end in strong claws.

Scientific Name
Phoca vitulina

Diet
Carnivorous

Living Environment
Water

Conservation Status
Least concern

29

RAT

IT HAS HIGHLY DEVELOPED SENSES

There are about 65 species, with the brown rat and the black rat being the ones with the widest global distribution.

THEY HAVE HIGHLY DEVELOPED SENSES OF SMELL AND TASTE.

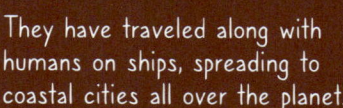
They have traveled along with humans on ships, spreading to coastal cities all over the planet.

They have a long tail that helps them to keep their balance and control their movement while jumping. Their tail is as long as their body.

They have a keen sense of hearing, allowing them to easily detect danger and evade predators.

THEIR EARS ARE BIG, BROAD, AND THIN.

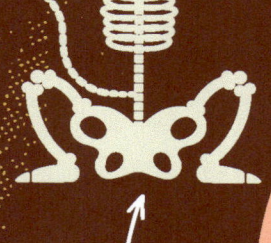

They have a flexible skeleton and an elongated body that allows them to fit through narrow holes.

Rats can move their eyes independently of each other.

Their hind legs are longer than the front legs and have 5 toes on each paw.

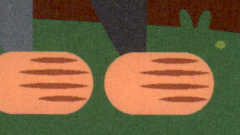
Their front legs are short, with 4 toes on each paw.

 Scientific Name **Rattus**	 Diet **Omnivorous**	 Living Environment **Land and Water**	 Conservation Status **Least concern**

They catch their prey by climbing skillfully: they can climb up the smoothest walls and walk along pipes, cables, branches, and ropes.

They are exceptional swimmers, and can catch small fish, crabs, snails, and aquatic insects.

THEY LIVE IN COMMUNITIES AND ARE VERY TERRITORIAL.

They capture their prey with their front paws and kill it with their teeth.

THEIR PREDATORY INSTINCT IS ACTIVATED ONLY WHEN HUNGRY.

HABITAT
Forests, grasslands, mountains, fields, deserts, river banks, urban areas, and environments with human-made buildings.

GEOGRAPHIC DISTRIBUTION

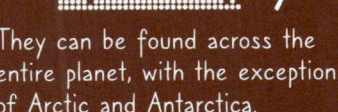

They are very cunning: they plan their attacks as a team and can snatch eggs from nests without breaking them.

They can be found across the entire planet, with the exception of Arctic and Antarctica.

They also eat eggs, chicks, and sleeping animals.

They feed on fruit, roots, small mammals, reptiles, insects, carrion, and garbage.

REPRODUCTION
They can have pups up to **6 TIMES A YEAR.**

Gestation lasts approximately **23 DAYS.**

They usually give birth to between **4 AND 8 PUPS PER LITTER.**

Their fur is thick and soft. It can be gray, brown, black, pale yellow, or white, depending on the species.

They have 2 lower and 2 upper incisors that are continuously growing to compensate for the wear from their constant gnawing.

The pups weigh less than **¼ AN OUNCE (7 GRAMS).**

UP TO **3** YEARS

UP TO **12** INCHES

UP TO **18** OUNCES

LIFE EXPECTANCY
They can live for up to 3 years.

They can grow to be 12 inches (30 centimeters) long.

The weight of Norway rats varies from 5 to 18 ounces (140 to 510 grams). Females are smaller than males.

Taxonomy
Phylum: **chordata**
Class: **mammalia**
Order: **rodentia**

THE COLOR OF THEIR FEATHERS CHANGES DEPENDING ON THE WAY THE LIGHT HITS THEM.

↓

They are well camouflaged in an environment of plants and water.

↓

Their colors are striking: blue, turquoise, green, gray, yellow, orange, and white.

UP TO **8** INCHES

They grow to be up to 8 inches (20 centimeters) in length.

UP TO **1½** OUNCES

Their average weight is about 1 to 1½ ounces (28 to 43 grams).

UP TO **10** YEARS

LIFE EXPECTANCY

Their lifespan ranges from 6 to 10 years.

Their wingspan is around 10 inches (25 centimeters)

10 inches

BILL
They have a black bill that is very large compared to their body.

MONOCULAR VISION
(in the air)

↓

Using each eye separately.

BINOCULAR VISION
(in the water)

↓

Using both eyes at once.

They measure the distance before diving down and catching their prey with their bill.

They can rotate their head to the side to see their prey.

THEIR FEET ARE STOCKY AND BRIGHTLY COLORED.

FEET

Taxonomy
Phylum: **chordata**
Class: **aves**
Order: **coraciiformes**

After catching their prey, they take it back to their perch to swallow it.

KINGFISHER

IT DIVES TO CATCH ITS PREY

There are 90 known species, divided into 3 groups: Alcedinidae, Halcyonidae, and Cerylidae.

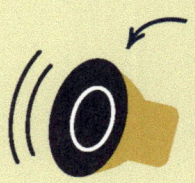

They make piercing sounds while flying and while resting.

THE KINGFISHER GETS ITS NAME BECAUSE IT'S SO GOOD AT CATCHING FISH. IT'S THE KING OF THE FISHERMEN.

FISH MAKES UP A LARGE PART OF THEIR DIET.

They also feed on aquatic insects, reptiles (such as snakes), amphibians, crustaceans, and small mammals.

THEY GO ON MIGRATIONS TO GET AWAY FROM THE WINTER.

Males travel shorter distances than females.

REPRODUCTION

They dig tunnels in the sides of cliffs or in the banks of rivers or bodies of water.

The tunnels can be up to 6 feet (1.8 meters) long.

THEY LAY BETWEEN 6 AND 7 EGGS.

Incubation lasts between 19 and 21 days. The chicks are ready to leave the nest 23 to 27 days after hatching.

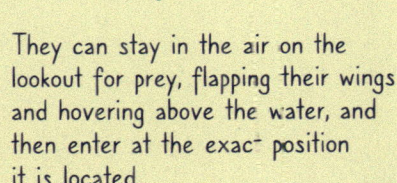

They can stay in the air on the lookout for prey, flapping their wings and hovering above the water, and then enter at the exact position it is located.

WHEN HUNTING, THEY PERCH ON TREE BRANCHES NEAR STREAMS, RIVERS, LAKES, OR LAGOONS, FROM WHERE THEY CAN LOCATE FISH.

HABITAT

Coastal areas of rivers, marshes, ponds, reservoirs, lagoons, lakes, estuaries, and marine coasts.

GEOGRAPHIC DISTRIBUTION

They can be found in Europe, Africa, and Asia.

Scientific Name
Alcedo atthis

Diet
Omnivorous

Living Environment
Air

Conservation Status
Least concern

DRAGONFLY
IT CATCHES ITS PREY IN FLIGHT

The oldest fossil is from the Carboniferous Period, about 320 million years ago.

There are more than 6,400 species.

They have strong jaws to crush their prey.

THEY HAVE LARGE COMPOUND EYES AND EXCELLENT VISION. THE CAN SEE IN ALL DIRECTIONS AT ONCE.

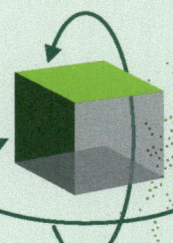

WINGS →
They have elongated, thin, strong, and membranous wings.

They're able to flap their wings in different ways to regulate their flight speed.

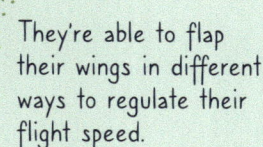

LEGS
They have 6 legs, which are covered in tiny hairs.

80%
of their brain is dedicated to analyzing visual information.

BODY →
They have a hard and rigid body.

GEOGRAPHIC DISTRIBUTION

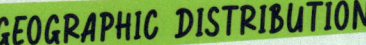

They can be found on all continents with warm and semi-warm climates.

HABITAT
Areas near lakes, rivers, ponds, lagoons, wetlands, and marshes.

THEY CAN SEE THEIR PREY FROM A DISTANCE OF UP TO 39 FEET (12 METERS).

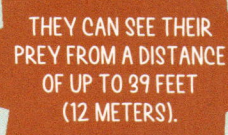

They exhibit a variety of colors: blue, green, yellow, violet, brown, and black.

Taxonomy
Phylum: **arthropoda**
Class: **insecta**
Order: **odonata**

THEY CATCH THEIR PREY 95% OF THE TIME.

UP TO 7 YEARS

THE WINGSPAN IS UP TO
6 inches
(15 centimeters)

They can fly at a speed of 53 miles per hour (85 kilometers per hour).

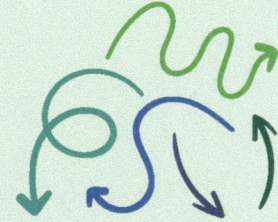

While flying, they can remain stationary; they can move backwards, upwards, or downwards, and can make sharp turns at high speed.

They use optical illusions to stalk other insects that invade their territory.

LIFE EXPECTANCY
Their lifespan can range from 3 months to 7 years.

UP TO 5 INCHES
They can be between 1 and 5 inches (2.5 and 13 centimeters) in length.

UP TO 0.04 OUNCES
Their average weight is up to 0.04 ounces (1.1 grams).

Their head and body can move independently.

They can move in such a way that they project themselves as a static object while rapidly attacking their prey.

THEY HUNT CONTINUOUSLY, CLEARING THE AIR OF INSECTS.

They feed on mosquitoes, flies, bees, and butterflies.

They catch their prey from below, attacking them with their legs.

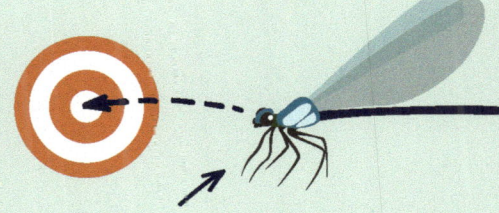

The head keeps their prey in sight, while the body maneuvers to get itself in the best angle to capture it.

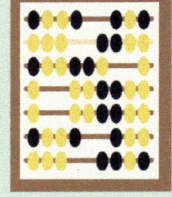

They are very intelligent: they have a great capacity for learning and improving their hunting techniques.

REPRODUCTION
The female lays her eggs in the water or near it, on floating plants.

The eggs hatch into nymphs that feed on mosquito larvae.

This period can last between
2 MONTHS AND 5 YEARS.

The nymph undergoes its metamorphosis to become an adult and begins to fly.

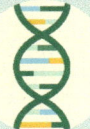 Scientific Name **Anisoptera**

 Diet **Carnivorous**

 Living Environment **Air**

 Conservation Status **Least concern**

UP TO 16 YEARS

LIFE EXPECTANCY
The oldest swordfish to date was 16 years old.

UP TO 10 FEET

They can grow to be between 7 and 10 feet (2.1 and 3 meters) in length.

UP TO 1,400 POUNDS

The heaviest swordfish we know of weighed in at 1,400 pounds (635 kilograms).

HOMEOTHERM
Their body temperature depends on the ambient temperature.

ECTOTHERM
However, they can regulate the temperature of some organs themselves.

They stay deep underwater during the day and come up to the surface at night.

They swim at a depth of **600 TO 2,600 FEET (183 TO 792 METERS).**

DORSAL FIN

BILL

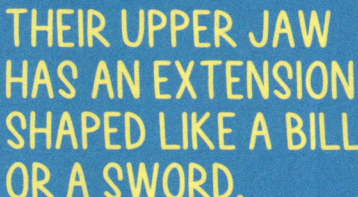

THEIR UPPER JAW HAS AN EXTENSION SHAPED LIKE A BILL OR A SWORD.

They have dark blue coloring on their back and a silvery, gray, or light brown belly.

PECTORAL FINS

62 MPH

They can reach a speed of 62 miles per hour (100 kilometers per hour).

Specimens from the Pacific Ocean grow to be larger than those from the Atlantic Ocean and the Mediterranean Sea.

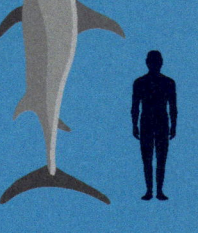

SWORDFISH
IT STUNS ITS PREY WITH ITS SWORD

Taxonomy
Phylum: **chordata**
Class: **actinopterygii**
Order: **istiophoriformes**

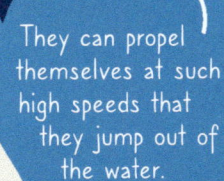

They can propel themselves at such high speeds that they jump out of the water.

THEY ARE AGILE AND CAN MOVE VERY QUICKLY.

They use their sword as a weapon to attack their prey.

They swim around schools of fish, before hitting them with their sword to stun, distract, and then eat them.

A solitary and migratory fish, they move between warm and cold waters in search of food.

They can swallow a fish whole, though they sometimes cut them into pieces.

DORSAL FIN

TAIL FIN

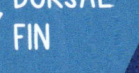

They feed on barracudas, mackerel, hake, tuna, squid, and various types of crustacea.

ANAL FINS

They have a cylindrical, streamlined body that is narrow at the tip.

GEOGRAPHIC DISTRIBUTION

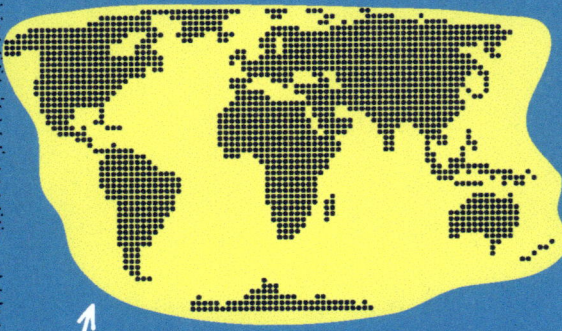

They can be found in all oceans of the world.

HABITAT

Open waters with strong ocean currents. They prefer tropical, subtropical, and temperate waters.

REPRODUCTION
OVIPAROUS

Occurs in warm waters.

The female lays eggs and the male swims around and fertilizes them.

When they hatch the fish is about **⅙ OF AN INCH (4 MILLIMETERS) LONG.**

As they grow, the body becomes narrower and more streamlined.

Scientific Name
Xiphias gladius

Diet
Carnivorous

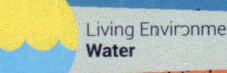
Living Environment
Water

Conservation Status
Endangered

COMMON RAVEN

IT CLEVERLY ADAPTS TO SITUATIONS

The genus of ravens and crows (Corvus) includes over 40 species, which vary in terms of the shape of their tails, the thickness of their beaks, and their communication strategies.

BEAK

Their beak is black, strong, robust, and curved.

Their eyes are dark brown as adults and grayish blue when they are young.

Their feathers are jet black with iridescent blue and purple reflections.

UP TO 27 INCHES

It can grow to be between 19 and 27 inches (48 and 69 centimeters) long.

The feathers of the extinct subspecies pied raven where white to gray on the belly and head.

UP TO 15 YEARS

LIFE EXPECTANCY

They live for between 10 and 15 years.

MORE THAN 4 POUNDS

They can weigh more than 4 pounds (1.8 kilograms).

Crows from colder regions are larger than those from warmer regions.

THEIR TAIL FEATHERS ARE LONGER THAN THE REST.

THEIR WINGSPAN IS

45–51 INCHES
(114–130 CENTIMETERS).

Taxonomy
Phylum: **chordata**
Class: **aves**
Order: **passeriformes**

THEY HAVE ONE OF THE LARGEST BRAINS OF ALL BIRD SPECIES.

They are able to imitate sounds, the songs of other birds, and even single human words.

When flying, they emit a very characteristic caw.

CAW! CAW!

THEY ARE EXTREMELY INTELLIGENT.

They are capable of establishing friendships, communicating with each other, making tools from stones and sticks, remembering who harmed them, solving problems, and performing rituals similar to funerals.

They are very social birds, and their families tend to be united. They sleep in groups of up to

200 birds.

THEY EAT MORE ON COLD DAYS THAN ON WARM ONES.

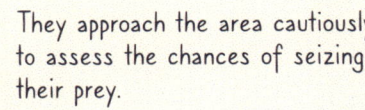

When hunting, they look for food in pairs, cooperating to get the prey to come out of its dwelling or nest.

They approach the area cautiously to assess the chances of seizing their prey.

They feed on carrion, small animals, amphibians, fish, eggs, the chicks of other birds, seeds, and fruit.

They look for food that is easy to catch.

REPRODUCTION

They are monogamous. The male and female use the same nest several times.

The female lays 3 to 7 eggs, which she incubates for 21 days.

21

The chicks leave the nest **5 TO 6 WEEKS** after birth.

GEOGRAPHIC DISTRIBUTION

They can be found in North and Central America, Europe, and large parts of Asia.

HABITAT

Mountains, boreal forests, coastal cliffs, tundra, semi-desert, and rural areas.

SEA OTTER

HUNTS WITH ITS FRONT PAWS

There are 3 recognized subspecies, which have different distribution areas.

Sea otters produce an intense odor when they are frightened.

Apart from the coastal otter, they belong to the only otter species that lives in the sea.

THEY HAVE A VERY THICK AND WATERPROOF COAT OF FUR.

This retains a layer of air between the fur and skin that acts as insulation.

Their fur is brown on the back and gray on the belly.

UP TO 20 YEARS

LIFE EXPECTANCY
Sea otters can live for 15 to 20 years.

ALMOST 5 FEET

They can grow to be almost 5 feet (1.5 meters) long.

UP TO 100 POUNDS

They can weigh between 30 and 100 pounds (14 and 45 kilograms).

Females are smaller than males.

Their body is elongated and muscular, with short legs.

150 FEET

They can dive to a depth of 150 feet (46 meters) to catch their prey.

Taxonomy
Phylum: **chordata**
Class: **mammalia**
Order: **carnivora**

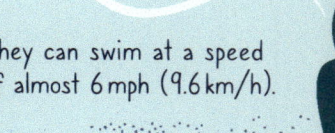

6 MPH They can swim at a speed of almost 6 mph (9.6 km/h).

HABITAT

Rocky seashores, shallow waters with seaweed, coral reefs, and coastal waters between 50 and 75 feet (15 and 23 meters) deep.

GEOGRAPHIC DISTRIBUTION

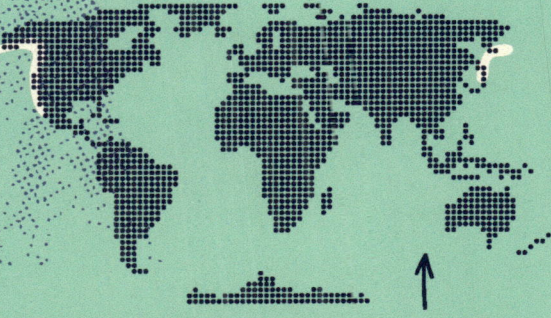

They can be found in the North Pacific Ocean, from Japan to Baja California, Mexico.

REPRODUCTION

Once mating is complete, gestation can last

6 TO 9 MONTHS.

A single pup is born, which will be nursed for between

4 AND 12 MONTHS.

THEY CAN DIVE FOR UP TO 5 MINUTES IN SEARCH OF FOOD.

Up to 100

They remain close to the coast in same-sex groups of up to 100. They often wrap themselves in seaweed so that the ocean current doesn't drag them away.

They can use rocks as tools to open the shells of shellfish and clams.

They have small skin pouches under their front paws where they store food when they dive.

It has the densest fur of any mammal:

UP TO 150,000 HAIR FOLLICLES PER SQUARE INCH (6,5 SQUARE CENTIMETERS).

They often float on their backs and move around using their paws and tail as paddles.

They feed on sea urchins, crustaceans, mussels, clams, small fish, and starfish.

They can live their entire lives without leaving the water.

PAWS

Each paw has 5 digits with strong claws and membranes that help to propel them through the water.

TAIL

It is short, flat, and muscular.

	Scientific Name *Enhydra lutris*	 Diet **Carnivorous**	 Living Environment **Water**	 Conservation Status **Endangered**

41

GEOGRAPHIC DISTRIBUTION

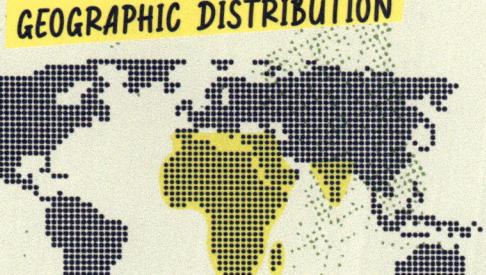

They can be found in Africa, Madagascar, southern Europe, Sri Lanka, southern India, and Asia.

HABITAT

Forests, mountains, lush forests, deserts, and steppes.

There are fossils of chameleons that are 13 to 23 million years old.

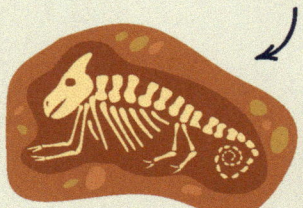

They have no ears. They detect sound frequencies through vibrations in the air.

THEIR EYES HAVE TELESCOPIC VISION AND CAN SEE 360 DEGREES AROUND THEM. EACH EYE CAN ALSO MOVE INDEPENDENTLY.

½ mile

They can see clearly up to a distance of more than half a mile (0.8 kilometers).

Some have horns on their heads, long crests, or ridges on their noses.

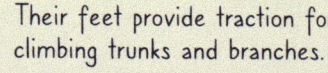

Their feet provide traction for climbing trunks and branches.

UP TO 28 INCHES

They can measure between less than 1 inch and 28 inches (2.5 and 71 centimeters) in length.

UP TO 18 OUNCES

They can weigh from less than 1 ounce to more than 18 ounces (28 to 500 grams).

Males are larger and have more striking coloring than females.

UP TO 15 YEARS

LIFE EXPECTANCY

Their life expectancy is between 5 and 15 years.

✗ FRONT LEGS

Their toes are divided into 2 groups, with 2 outer toes and 3 inner toes.

✗ HIND LEGS

They have 3 outer toes and 2 inner toes.

CHAMELEON

HUNTS USING ITS FAST TONGUE

There are about 200 species.

↓ ↓ ↓

40 PERCENT OF THE SPECIES LIVE ON THE ISLAND OF MADAGASCAR.

Their skin is hard, with scales and pigmentation that allow it to change color.

A FEW SECONDS.

It takes only a few seconds for them to change color. Color change is used for

COMMUNICATION, REPRODUCTION, DEFENSE CAMOUFLAGE, AND INTIMIDATION.

Taxonomy
Phylum: **chordata**
Class: **reptilia**
Order: **squamata**

The tip of their tongue is like a wet suction cup that traps prey.

It only takes 20 milliseconds for them to launch their tongue and eat an insect.

THEY MOVE VERY SLOWLY.

THEIR TONGUE IS STICKY AND RETRACTABLE. IT IS LONGER THAN THEIR ENTIRE BODY.

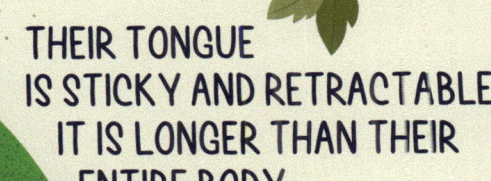

When hunting, they remain motionless while waiting for prey. They detect it in silence and launch their tongue.

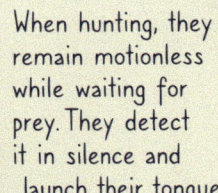

It has a prehensile tail that can support the weight of the body.

REPRODUCTION
THEY ARE OVIPAROUS.

↓

2-85 EGGS

They lay 2 to 85 eggs, depending on the species.

↓

The eggs hatch mostly within 4 to 12 months.

They have a technique to appear larger in front of their enemies: they reduce their width, elevating their spine, expanding their throat, and coiling their tail.

Depending on the species they feed on insects, small mammals, birds, sprouts, flowers, and fruit.

The female lays her eggs in a hole in the ground.

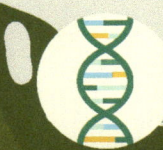
Scientific Name
Chamaeleonidae

Diet
Omnivorous

Living Environment
Land

Conservation Status
Endangered

EVERYBODY HUNTS

Life in the wild is a constant fight for survival. Nevertheless, all living creatures in an ecosystem are interdependent: Plant leaves, for example, are eaten by caterpillars. Caterpillars, in turn, are on the menu for frogs, and frogs are eaten by birds of prey such as eagles. So none of the animals could survive without the others or without plants.

There are many different hunting methods in the animal world, and some of them are used by the same animal.

Traps / Decoys / Camouflage
Some predators build traps that go unnoticed by the eyes of potential prey, or use decoys that lead their victims to a place where they can be ambushed. They also use camouflage to disappear into their surroundings.

Crocodile

Wasp

Alone / In Groups
Predators that act alone prefer to hunt alone as well, which improves their chances of capturing their prey. Predators that hunt in groups are highly social and work together to stalk their prey from different directions.

Bear

Puma

Ambush / Pursuit
Ambush predators conserve energy by remaining hidden and waiting patiently for their prey to approach. They capture their prey by stealth. Pursuit predators actively chase their prey until they get exhausted.

Snake

Squid

Ground / Air
Birds that hunt on the ground wait on the ground until their victim gets distracted, so they can pounce on them. Those that hunt in the air spot their prey from above and wait for the right moment to strike

Flamingo

Swift

TO FIND OUT MORE...

National Geographic Kids
natgeokids.com

American Museum of Natural History
amnh.org/explore/ology

WWF
worldwildlife.org

Greenpeace
greenpeace.org/international

Animals that hunt and eat other animals (prey) in order to survive are called predators. Many animals are closely connected through this predator-prey relationship.

Seahorse

Octopus

Spider

Army ant

Hyena

Dolphin

Frog

Jaguar

Starfish

Fox

Great white shark

Owl

Swan

Stork

Duck

Hawk

Traps/Decoys/Camouflage

Alone / In Groups

Ambush / Pursuit

Ground / Air

Defenders of Wildlife
defenders.org

IFAW
ifaw.org

Humane Society Europe
hsi-europe.org

IUCN Red List of Threatened Species
iucnredlist.org